# THE
# MERMAID
# AND
# THE WHALE

By Georgess McHargue

PICTURES BY ROBERT ANDREW PARKER

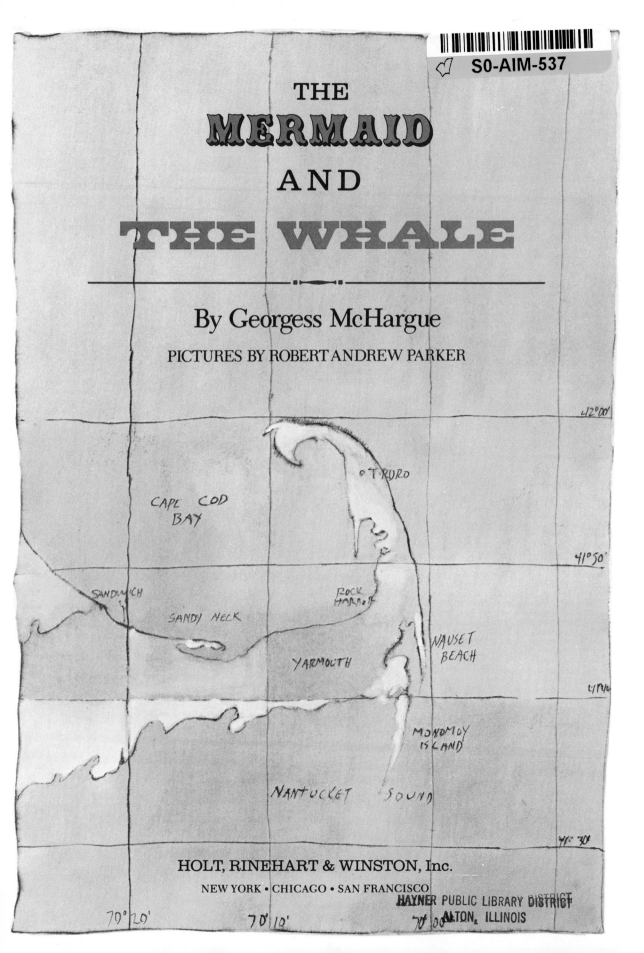

42°00'

o TRURO

CAPE COD
BAY

41°50'

SANDWICH

ROCK
HARBOR

SANDY NECK

NAUSET
BEACH

YARMOUTH

41°40'

MONOMOY
ISLAND

NANTUCKET SOUND

41°30'

**HOLT, RINEHART & WINSTON, Inc.**

NEW YORK · CHICAGO · SAN FRANCISCO

70°20'       70°10'       70°00'

LIBRARY OF CONGRESS CATALOGING
IN PUBLICATION DATA

McHargue, Georgess.
    The mermaid and the whale.

    SUMMARY: Recounts a mermaid's determined ef-
forts to win the love of a whale.

    [1. Folklore—United States] I. Parker, Robert
Andrew, illus. II. Title.
PZ8.1.M18Me        398.2'1'0973  [E]        73-7169
ISBN 0-03-011166-8

A HOLT REINFORCED EDITION

For Roger and Sarah H. and
Robert C. from the F. G.
(G. McHargue)

For My Mother and Father
(R. A. Parker)

IN WHALING DAYS, off Sandwich town in the state of Massachusetts, there lived a Mermaid. She played happily with the fish among the kelp fronds and liked to admire her silver scales and green hair in the tide pools along the shore.

Then one day the Mermaid fell in love. She fell in love with a finback whale who had come to live in the waters off Lost Island. His name was Long John, and a finer, faster, cannier whale than he had not been sighted in those parts for many years. Long John had left his old sounding-ground up Truro way because he suspected his luck was running out. He had outsmarted every whalemaster in the area, flapped his flukes and swum away smiling, but now he thought a change of scene might be good for his health.

However, Long John soon found that his new life was not all spouting and basking either. He was a loner, who liked nothing better than to cruise by himself far out of sight of land or even of the curious seagulls. Yet now, wherever he went there was the Mermaid.

She offered him clam cakes. She wooed him with kelp chowder. She begged him to give her a ride on his back. She teased him and ogled him and flattered him fish-eyed with her admiration of his mighty sides, his noble brow, his melting eyes.

When Long John refused to pay any attention to her, the Mermaid grew cunning. She went to the clams, lobsters, crabs and oysters. By threatening to guide the clammers and lobstermen to their hiding places, she persuaded them to help her.

On a warm summer day when Long John was just lazing about near the sea bottom, hardly flicking a fin, all the shellfish in the area jumped onto his broad flat tail at once. The Mermaid hoped that more than a ton of assorted sea creatures would hold the whale still so she could talk to him without getting out of breath from chasing him.

That was a day long remembered in the undersea history of the Sandwich coast. Off went Long John on a driving, diving whale-dash, over wave and under water, until every one of his passengers lost hold and there was a trail of dizzy shellfish halfway to Yarmouth. It was a very long claw-walk back to the rocks around Lost Island and by the time they got home many of the travelers were not speaking to the Mermaid.

But she, although disappointed, was by no means ready to give up. Thereafter she spent much of her time sitting on the rocks and fashioning a very large harness of woven kelp strands. It was about the right size to bridle a whale.

The Mermaid also did some thinking as she sat. One fine afternoon she left her work and swam upcoast to Truro. There by the water, on Truro Coomb, she found Ichabod Paddock. The greatest whalemaster of his time was Ichabod Paddock, the same man who was later sent to Nantucket and Martha's Vineyard to teach the ignorant islanders the art of catching fish. Ichabod had his spyglass in his hand and was peering off toward the horizon, looking for a ship that was due to bring him some inheritance money from England. Then he saw a swirl of green and silver and the Mermaid looked up at him smiling.

"Howdy-do," said Ichabod.

"Evenin," answered the Mermaid, who knew how to be polite when it suited her. Then she wasted no words in saying what she had come for. She told Ichabod how Long John, the only whale who ever lived to laugh at him, had moved down to Lost Island. She played on the whalemaster's vanity and also on his greed, offering him ropes of pearls and baskets of coral if he would agree to catch Long John for her. Ichabod, however, was looking forward to a comfortable retirement as soon as his ship came in, and he refused. The Mermaid then became more pressing. She offered him sunken treasure, even the famous copper box full of gold bars that folk say lies off Monomoy. But still Ichabod was wary. He had heard that Mermaids' gifts often turn to water at the first full moon.

Finally the Mermaid offered love. She held out her gleaming arms to the whalemaster and sang bewitchingly,

Oh, love is kind to the least of men,
Hi and lo, hi and lo,
Though he be but a drunken tar,
Hi and lo, away.

Far from land and the sight of land,
Hi and lo, hi and lo,
Oh, who will love the sailor man?
Hi and lo, away.

Ichabod was stirred to his soul, for the song was a magical one with sea lore in it. However, he was just able to remind himself that a Mermaid's love is as unreliable as her gifts. Besides, he was insulted by the remarks in the song's first verse, for he considered that he never took a drop more rum than he should. Therefore he refused again. But still the Mermaid pestered him and pleaded with him until he realized he would have to do something to free himself of this deep-sea nuisance.

"Very well, ma'am," he said to the Mermaid, "I'll do this for ye. Tell Long John that Whalemaster Ichabod Paddock will never raise harpoon against him again if he will take you on his back and ride you once around the Cape." And Ichabod tipped his hat to her and went away home.

The Mermaid lost no time in making for home also.

The next day she took two squid-hound bass with her as witnesses to the whalemaster's statement, and went to see Long John, feeling sure that this time she could win his heart.

When the great finback heard about Ichabod's promise he was secretly relieved, for he was more afraid of the whalemaster than he liked to admit. To seal the bargain the whale allowed the Mermaid to bridle him with her kelp rope and take her ride then and there. "Git aboard," he invited her, "and set yourself up for'ard."

As lovely as a sea lily, the Mermaid curled herself on the whale's forehead, and so busy was she with holding onto the harness and enjoying her triumph that she never noticed the wink Long John gave the bass-fish as they started off.

Upcoast and around past Nauset beach they cruised, Long John as tame as a shrimp. Back and forth he tacked, as if he were a frigate with the Mermaid at the helm. The astonished squawks of the gulls blended with the sound of the Mermaid's jubilant singing. She sang "Sailing, Sailing, Over the Bounding Main," "Cape Cod Girls," and "Blow Ye Winds in the Morning," to celebrate her victory. (For of course she had no intention of freeing Long John from his harness once the ride was over.)

As the sun was setting, they came about by the Peaked Hill Bars and headed back across the broad Bay toward Sandwich. The whale was certainly giving the Mermaid her money's worth of riding.

Suddenly, however, Long John dove under the water and took off as if on a compass course straight for the Sandwich shore. When he got so close in that he was almost scraping bottom, he surfaced and spouted high and handsome. Up went the Mermaid on the jet—up and up.

No longer whale-riding, she was sky-riding, and the light of the rising moon gleamed silver on her scales. The townsfolk thought it had begun to rain as she scattered sea drops in the streets. Over the housetops she sailed, then made a splash-landing in Sandwich Pond while Long John sped off for freedom and open water.

The Mermaid is still in Sandwich Pond, they say. The little stream that runs out by the mill dam is far too shallow for her to swim back to the sea. Now she has ducks for friends and has given up whale-chasing.

But sometimes, on moonlit nights, those who pass the pond may glimpse a gleam of silver and hear a voice like a wet echo singing the end of an old song:

And we never caught that whale,
        Brave boys,
We never caught that whale...

As for Long John, he disappeared from those parts long ago. But before he went, he scraped and squirmed out of the seaweed harness that had been fastened on him. Even today, great kelpy ropes of it wash up on the shore near Sandwich, so that anyone who wants to can own a piece of the Mermaid's bridle.

## AUTHOR'S NOTE

The story of the Mermaid and the Whale is an anonymous sailor's yarn popular on Cape Cod a century ago and more. It was first recorded in print by Elizabeth Reynard in *The Narrow Land, Folk Chronicles of Old Cape Cod* in 1934. However, parts of the story must already have been influenced by the Indian tale of Squant the Seawoman, a very much older tradition which the early settlers learned from their Indian neighbors. Local history is also reflected in another way, for Ichabod Paddock was a real whalemaster who sailed out of Truro.

The grist mill whose dam forms one end of Sandwich Pond, otherwise known as Shawme Lake, was built sometime between the town's founding in 1637 and 1654, so the pond would certainly have been there to receive the Mermaid at the time of the story. However, at that time she would not have had such a long trip by air, since Sandwich Harbor stretched considerably farther inland than it does today.

## ABOUT THE AUTHOR

Georgess McHargue discovered the story of *The Mermaid and the Whale* while doing research for her much acclaimed book, *The Impossible People*. Before writing her version of this tale, she made a trip to Sandwich, Massachusetts, visited the pond, and consulted old maps of the area which revealed that the seacoast had moved since whaling days.

Ms. McHargue was born in Norwalk, Connecticut, and graduated from Radcliffe College. She is the author of nine books for young people, including four picture books. Among her hobbies are horticulture, wilderness camping, and travel. She now lives in Cambridge, Massachusetts, where she devotes much of her time to research in folklore and myth, her major field of study.

## ABOUT THE ARTIST

Robert Andrew Parker is the illustrator of a Caldecott Honor Book, *Pop Corn and Ma Goodness,* and other outstanding books for children. Some of his paintings are included in the collections of the Museum of Modern Art and the Whitney Museum. He lives with his wife and five sons in Carmel, New York.

## ABOUT THE BOOK

The text and display for this book were set in a combination of film typefaces, including Caledonia, Clarendon, Celtic Ornate, and Giorgio. The artist used ink and acrylic paints to prepare his full-color paintings, which were then camera-separated for printing by offset.

C